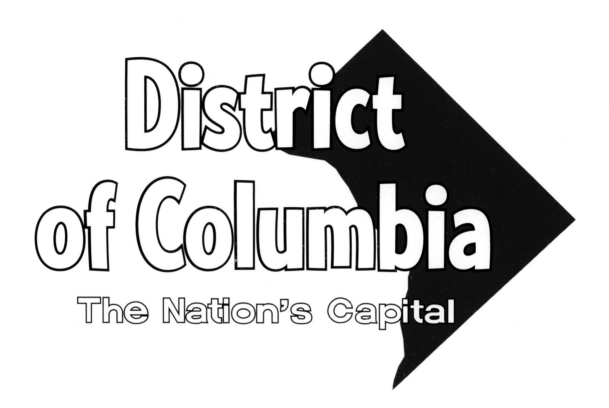

District of Columbia

The Nation's Capital

Marcia Amidon Lusted

PowerKiDS
press™
New York

Published in 2011 by The Rosen Publishing Group, Inc.
29 East 21st Street, New York, NY 10010

First Edition

Editor: Maggie Murphy
Book Design: Kate Laczynski
Photo Researcher: Jessica Gerweck

Photo Credits: Cover Lester Lefkowitz/Getty Images; pp. 5, 11, 17, 19, 22 (bird) Shutterstock.com; p. 7 MPI/Getty Images; p. 9 Washington Bureau/Getty Images; p. 13 Panoramic Images/Getty Images; p. 15 Alex Wong/Getty Images; p. 22 (tree) DEA/C. Sappa/Getty Images; p. 22 (flower) Brian Leatart/Getty Images; p. 22 (Duke Ellington) Metronome/Getty Images; p. 22 (Connie Chung) Amy Sussman/Getty Images; p. 22 (Al Gore) Dr. Billy Ingram/WireImage/Getty Images.

Library of Congress Cataloging-in-Publication Data

Lusted, Marcia Amidon.
   District of Columbia : the nation's capital / Marcia Amidon Lusted. — 1st ed.
      p. cm. — (Our amazing states)
   Includes bibliographical references and index.
   ISBN 978-1-4488-0667-6 (library binding) — ISBN 978-1-4488-0772-7 (pbk.) —
ISBN 978-1-4488-0773-4 (6-pack)
   1. Washington (D.C.)— Juvenile literature. I. Title.
   F194.3.L87 2011
   975.3—dc22
                                        2010003467

Manufactured in the United States of America

CPSIA Compliance Information: Batch #WS10PK: For Further Information contact Rosen Publishing, New York, New York at 1-800-237-9932

Contents

More than a City

It is more than just a city, but it is not a state. It is also one of the most important places in our country. What is this place? It is the District of Columbia, also known as Washington, D.C. The District of Columbia is the capital of the entire United States.

Washington, D.C., is shaped like a diamond. It is located on the **border** of Maryland and Virginia. It sits beside the Potomac River, not far from the coast of the Atlantic Ocean.

The District of Columbia is home to around 600,000 people, as well as 174 foreign **embassies**. One of the most famous people to make their home there is the president of the United States, who lives at 1600 Pennsylvania Avenue.

Here, fireworks are shown above the Lincoln Memorial (left), the Washington Monument (center), and the Capitol (right) during the District of Columbia's annual Fourth of July celebration.

City on Fire

Hundreds of years before the city was built, the Nacotchtank peoples of the Algonquian Native Americans lived in the present-day District of Columbia. One of the first European **explorers** to the area, Captain John Smith, came in 1608. In 1790, President George Washington **inspected** different places on the Potomac River where a new capital city could be built. He chose the land that is now the District of Columbia.

The city of Washington, D.C., was carefully planned. By 1800, it was the official capital of the United States. However, during the War of 1812, British troops occupied Washington and set fire to the city. They burned the Capitol, the White House, and the Treasury, as well as other public buildings.

This drawing shows British soldiers setting fire to Washington, D.C., on August 24, 1814, during the War of 1812. This event is sometimes called the Burning of Washington.

From the Civil War to Civil Rights

During the Civil War, Washington, D.C., became a military base for Union soldiers. After the war was over, the city grew quickly. Many new government buildings were built.

As the capital of the United States, Washington, D.C., became a center for protests during the American **civil rights movement**. In 1963, 250,000 people marched in Washington to support a new civil rights bill proposed by President John F. Kennedy. There Dr. Martin Luther King Jr. gave a famous speech, called the "I have a dream" speech.

Today the District of Columbia is still one of the country's most important cities. There, the federal government is run. Places such as the National **Archives preserve** our history, too.

Dr. Martin Luther King Jr. is shown here in Washington, D.C., on August 28, 1963. Every year, Americans celebrate Dr. King's birthday on the third Monday in January.

A City from Two States

The land where Washington, D.C., sits was once part of both Maryland and Virginia. Back then, it was mostly farmland and tree-covered hills, with some **wetlands**. The city also has many gentle sloping hills. The most famous one is Capitol Hill, where the Capitol sits.

Washington, D.C., is bordered by the Potomac River, which runs into Chesapeake Bay and then to the Atlantic Ocean. The Tidal Basin, which is part of the river, is a large pool beside the National Mall and the Jefferson Memorial. It is ringed with cherry trees, which blossom every spring.

Summers in Washington are very hot and **humid**. While it gets more rain than snow in the winter, the city can be very cold then.

Here, you can see the slope of Capitol Hill, with the U.S. Capitol at the top. Before the Capitol was built there, the hill was called Jenkins Hill.

Land of Cherry Blossoms

Because almost all of the District of Columbia is a city, very few wild animals are found there. However, the city does have Rock Creek National Park, where coyotes, raccoons, owls, foxes, and deer live. Bird-watchers can see cardinals, woodpeckers, wrens, and goldfinches there. **Migrant** birds often stop there on their way south.

Washington, D.C., is famous for its cherry trees, which bloom every spring around the Tidal Basin. More than 3,000 cherry blossom trees were planted in the city in 1912. The trees were a gift to the city from the country of Japan. The city celebrates their famous pink and white blossoms every spring during the National Cherry Blossom Festival.

The first National Cherry Blossom Festival was held in Washington, D.C., in 1935. Today, more than a million people visit the cherry blossoms around the Tidal Basin, shown here, every year.

What Do People Do in the District of Columbia?

In Washington, D.C., many people work for either the federal government or in a business that takes care of **tourists**. The government provides jobs for about 150,000 people in the city. They may work in government offices or agencies. Some people who work for the government actually live in other states and just stay in Washington for part of the year, such as U.S. **senators** and **representatives**.

The District of Columbia gets more than 20 million visitors a year. Some of the visitors are tourists there to see the sights, and others are diplomats and politicians. Many people work for businesses that provide food, a place to stay, or things to do for these visitors.

U.S. Attorney General Eric Holder (center) is one of the 150,000 Americans who work for the federal government in the District of Columbia. He works for the U.S. Department of Justice.

Climbing Capitol Hill

The city of Washington, D.C., is filled with famous buildings. One of the most important buildings in the city is the Capitol. In 1793, George Washington laid the cornerstone for the Capitol. The building was completely finished in 1863. The two wings of the building are home to the Senate and the House of Representatives. The Capitol shares Capitol Hill with the Supreme Court building and the Library of Congress. The National Mall, with its famous presidential **monuments**, stretches out from the foot of the Capitol.

The White House is another very famous building in Washington, D.C. Since 1800, all of America's presidents have lived there. Today it is a symbol of the presidency and the United States.

Here, you can see the outside of the Library of Congress. The library has the largest collection in the world. It includes nearly 142 million books, photographs, maps, and other things.

Visiting Washington, D.C.

Washington has many great places to visit. The National Mall is a strip of grassy lawn more than 2 miles (3 km) long that runs from Capitol Hill to the Potomac River. It is sometimes called America's Front Yard. Here you can find famous monuments, such as the Lincoln Memorial and the Vietnam Veterans Memorial. The Washington Monument, which is shaped like an **obelisk**, is also on the Mall. A reflecting pool stretches from the Lincoln Memorial back toward the Capitol.

The museums of the Smithsonian Institution are here, too, including the Air and Space Museum and the National Museum of American History. You can also visit the National Archives, where many documents and photos of American history are kept.

You can find this large statue of the sixteenth president of the United States, Abraham Lincoln, at the Lincoln Memorial, in Washington, D.C.

Come to the District of Columbia!

Whether you come to the District of Columbia as a tourist or live and work there every day, Washington, D.C., is a great place to be. You can see the cherry trees near the Jefferson Memorial, wander through the gardens at the National Arboretum, or visit the U.S. Holocaust Memorial Museum. You can hike the trails in Rock Creek Park or visit the nearby Arlington National Cemetery, where many famous Americans are buried. You can also have a picnic or play a game of Frisbee on the National Mall!

Whatever you do in Washington, D.C., remember that you are in one of the most important places in the United States. It is the capital of your country!

Glossary

archives (AR-kyvz) A place where records or historical documents are kept.

border (BOR-der) A line that separates two pieces of land.

civil rights movement (SIH-vul RYTS MOOV-mint) People and groups working together to win freedom and equality for all.

embassies (EM-buh-seez) Official homes and offices in a foreign country.

explorers (ek-SPLOR-erz) People who travel and look for new land.

humid (HYOO-med) Wet.

inspected (in-SPEK-ted) Checked over closely.

migrant (MY-grunt) Someone or something that moves from one place to another.

monuments (MON-yuh-mints) Things built to honor people or events.

obelisk (AH-buh-lisk) A tall post that ends in a triangular shape.

preserve (prih-ZURV) To keep something from being lost.

representatives (reh-prih-ZEN-tuh-tivz) People elected to serve in the House of Representatives, one of the law-making parts of the U.S. government.

senators (SEH-nuh-terz) People elected to serve in the Senate, one of the law-making parts of the U.S. government.

tourists (TUR-ists) People who take a trip or a tour for pleasure.

wetlands (WET-landz) Land with a lot of wetness in the soil.

District of Columbia Symbols

Tree
Scarlet Oak

Bird
Wood Thrush

Flower
American
Beauty Rose

Seal

Famous People from the District of Columbia

Duke Ellington
(1899–1974)
Born in Washington, D.C.
Jazz Musician

Connie Chung
(1946–)
Born in Washington, D.C.
News Anchor

Al Gore
(1948–)
Born in Washington, D.C.
U.S Vice President/
Nobel Peace Prize Winner

District of Columbia Map

Legend

⭐ Capital

〰 River

Rock Creek

White House

Supreme Court Building

National Mall

Capitol

Tidal Basin

Anacostia River

Potomac River

Memorial Parks

District of Columbia Facts

Population: About 591,833

Area: 68 square miles (176 sq km)

Motto: "Justice for All"

Song: "The Star-Spangled Banner," words by Francis Scott Key and music by John Stafford Smith

Index

Web Sites

Due to the changing nature of Internet links, PowerKids Press has developed an online list of Web sites related to the subject of this book. This site is updated regularly. Please use this link to access the list:

www.powerkidslinks.com/amst/dc/